Chuck

THE DIFFERENT VAMPIRE

BOOK ONE

by *Marla Paul - Merasty*
A.K.A. *Miss Marla*

Illustrated by Alan Margolis

Published by:

FriesenPress

Suite 300 – 852 Fort Street

Victoria, BC, Canada V8W 1H8

www.friesenpress.com

Distributed to the trade by The Ingram Book Company

Dedication

To my friend Shanon, who made me write my vision down on paper, and to my husband George and my boys Kaeden and Brenden who always showed support.

About the Author

Marla Paul - Merasty, A.K.A. Miss Marla, is married and a mother of two children. She is an Educational Assistant in Winnipeg, Manitoba, Canada. She wrote the book CHUCK because she had a dream about writing a book with a character named CHUCK. The next morning, her good friend told her to write down her dream and CHUCK became a reality.

3243

6

Hi! My name is CHUCK. I am a vampire. I was born in England 642 years ago. When I became a vampire, I was eleven years old. I will always act and feel as if I was eleven years old, but I am not! I am different. I am not like other vampires, I DON'T LIKE BLOOD, and have learned to live without it.

I like to be outside on sunny days, while all my friends and family sleep.

See, I told you I was different! How many vampires do you know that like to go out in the sun?

I couldn't always be outside in the sun, but one day, by pure accident, I learned of my power. While my family and friends slept, I jumped out of my coffin and I left our dark ten-storey warehouse and stood on the sunny sidewalk outside our building all by myself.

I started to feel achy, my muscles hurt, and my stomach twinged. You know how you feel when you get the flu? That feeling!

The day I learned of my power I was standing on the sidewalk amazed I was outside. An old lady dropped her cane in front of me. I picked it up and gave it to her.

"Thank you, young man," she said with a smile, and a wink of her eye.

I felt a warm, fuzzy feeling in my heart and I started to feel better, not achy! I decided to continue walking down the sidewalk. I walked and walked. It was amazing to be out in the sun! Then out of nowhere, I started to feel achy again. It was hard to even walk. I had no energy. I felt really tired!

A man walking beside me on the sidewalk sneezed. I said, "Bless you".

The man looked at me, and said, "Thank you, young man." Then he asked, "What is your name boy?"

I replied, "CHUCK". The man said, "Well CHUCK, I am glad to see you have manners", and he kept walking.

I felt that warm fuzzy feeling in my heart again, and I started to feel better. I wondered, does doing nice things for people and having manners make my heart feel fuzzy? Did this help me stay out in the sun during the day?

I continued to walk down the sidewalk. I walked and I walked and I walked. I walked for a longer time than before, and then I started to feel achy again. Then, all of a sudden, I saw her!

There was a girl about ten years old. She was in a wheelchair. She had a bag of groceries on her lap and she could not get her wheelchair over the curb to get on the sidewalk. I ran up and asked, "Can I help you?"

She said, "Yes, could you give me a little push to get my chair on the sidewalk please?" After she was on the sidewalk, she gratefully said, "Thank you! I haven't seen you before, do you live around here?"

I said, "Yes, back there in the warehouse".

She said, "My name is Alison. What's yours?"

I said, "CHUCK". Then I asked, "Why are you in a wheelchair?"

Alison told me she had Cerebral Palsy and she couldn't use her legs very well. Then she asked me if I wanted to have a play date tomorrow at the playground across the street. I said, "YES! What time?" She said, "One o'clock after lunch. Is that okay?" I said, "See you there!" I was so excited I ran all the way back to my warehouse.

I felt great! Having manners and helping people allowed me to stay in the sun. Being in the sun was fun! I loved that warm fuzzy feeling. I was so excited, I couldn't wait to tell my family about my day and my play date with Alison.

I opened the steel door to my loft, and my family was still asleep! So I jumped in my coffin and started to DAY DREAM about tomorrow.

THE END

What is Cerebral Palsy?

CEREBRAL = OF THE BRAIN

PALSY = LACK OF MUSCLE CONTROL

According to the Cerebral Palsy Association of Manitoba, Cerebral Palsy (CP) is a term used to describe a group of disorders affecting body movement and muscle coordination. The medical definition of CP is "A non-progressive but not unchanging disorder of movement and or posture, due to insult to or an anomaly of the developing brain."

Cerebral Palsy at its mildest may result in a slight awkwardness of movement or hand control.

At its most severe, CP may result in virtually no muscle control, profoundly affecting movement and speech.

You can't catch Cerebral Palsy and you don't get it from your birth parents. It is something that could happen to any of us. It is something that could happen when you're in your birth mom's tummy or when you're coming out of your birth mom's tummy. Here is an interesting fact; if you had Meningitis (a really bad virus) or brain hemorrhage (bleeding in the brain) or lack of oxygen to the brain when you were a child, you could get Cerebral Palsy.

*People with Cerebral Palsy are just like you or I. Sometimes everyday things that we do and take for granted can be a bit of a challenge for a person with CP and they might need a little help and understanding. For more information, go online and visit the Cerebral Palsy Association of Manitoba or a Cerebral Palsy Association close to where you live.

What Are Illustrations?

Illustrations are the pictures in a book that have been drawn by a person; the person who draws the pictures is called an Illustrator. Children's Books have many beautiful illustrations. We the readers don't always have to read words in a book. We can look at pictures and still learn about the book.

Can you answer these three Questions about the illustrations in this book?

1. What did you see on the old ladies cane?

2. Did you see a recycle bin in the park?

3. What are the statues of in front of Chuck's warehouse?

Answers: 1) A duck. 2) Yes. 3) Gargoyles.

 30

What Are Manners?

Every culture has certain customs or rituals they follow. In Canada we respect all cultures and their customs, but we seem to use some important words daily like: please, thank you; excuse me or just by saying hello to someone. When we eat we also use manners such as sitting on a chair properly and not eating with our mouths too full, so other people can not see what we are eating. We can also show manners and not even say a word. We can make eye contact, smile, wave, or pick up something that has been dropped. We do so many things in a day and when we use our manners, it makes us more considerate of other peoples feelings. It also makes our world a happier place to be.

CPSIA information can be obtained
at www.ICGtesting.com
Printed in the USA
LVIW011918291012
304980LV00002B